JOANNE FINDON

illustrations by

TED NASMITH

Stoddart Kids

Book design by Counterpunch/Linda Gustafson

We acknowledge the Canada Council for the Arts and the Ontario Arts Council for their support of our publishing program.

First published in Canada in 1994 by Lester Publishing Limited

Published in paperback in 1997 by Stoddart Kids,
a division of Stoddart Publishing Co. Limited
34 Lesmill Road
Toronto, Canada M3B 2T6
Tel (416) 445-3333 FAX (416) 445-5967
e-mail Customer.Service@ccmailgw.genpub.com

Published in the United States in 1998 by Stoddart Kids
85 River Rock Drive, Suite 202
Buffalo, New York 14207
Toll free 1-800-805-1083
e-mail gdsinc@genpub.com

Canadian Cataloguing in Publication Data
Findon, Joanne, 1957–
The dream of Aengus

ISBN 0-7737-5930-1

I. Nasmith, Ted. II. Title.

PS8561.I5387D73 1997 jC813'.54 C97-931201-9
PZ7.F56Dr 1997

Printed and bound in Hong Kong

For my parents, who allowed me to dream

J. F.

To my daughter, Sharyn, and my sons, Mikey and Colin

May you all fulfill your dreams

T. N.

Long ago, when immortals walked the hills of Ireland, there lived a girl named Caer. She had eyes like the night and hair like the sun and when she played her harp you would think the whole Earth sang.

But Caer lived under a strange enchantment. Her father was King Ethal of the Shee-mound at Navan, a sorcerer so powerful that only the Dagda was his equal. Because of King Ethal's fear that Caer would one day marry a mortal man, he laid a curse upon her. This was her fate – to live every other year in the form of a swan on the cold, empty shores of Loch Bél Dracon.

At first, Caer didn't mind being a swan. She loved being able to fly, and she had her handmaidens with her, twenty other snowy swans who shared her fate. But then one day a young man came to the shore.

He was tall, with hair like burnished copper and eyes the color of a summer sky. He sat on a rock, gazed at the swans, and smiled. Then he began to sing a slow, haunting song.

"This is the man I could love," said Caer to her handmaidens as his rich, resonant voice spun a web of joy around her.

"Do not set your heart on him," they warned. "He is a mortal, and what mortal man would choose a wife who will fly from his side every other year?"

"Who is he?" Caer asked.

"He is Aengus, the son of King Leary of Ulster."

"I will find a way to come to him," she said, and she beat her wings and rose in the air. She circled the place where Aengus sat and let one long white feather drop at his feet. He paused in his song only long enough to pick up the feather and hold it up to the sun.

Aengus returned to the shores of the lake many times that year. But Caer's heart was heavy, for she could not speak to him.

The next year, when Caer was a girl at home again, she told her mother about the young man.

"What shall I do?" she whispered. "Father will never allow me to leave here in my human form."

"There is one way," said her mother. "I know an ancient spell that will allow you to enter Aengus's dreams. You may use it only when you are a swan, and you will not be able to speak to him, yet he will see your true form. But your father must never know!"

Caer carefully learned the spell by heart.

On Samain eve, the last night of the old year, Caer and her handmaidens filed out into the courtyard. They raised their arms to the sky and, out of the rising wind, clouds of feathers descended upon them. They beat their wings and rose in the air. By the light of the rising moon, Caer and the swan maidens sped like the wind toward Loch Bél Dracon.

That first night on the lake, as Caer floated on the moonlit water, she thought of the tall young man. In her mind she repeated the words of the spell. Slowly, slowly, the moonlight faded into a swirling mist and the mist darkened into the dimness of a room with one rushlight burning. There he was, Aengus of the copper hair, lying asleep on his bed.

"How I wish I could speak with him!" thought Caer.

Then she noticed a harp slung over the bedpost. She lifted the instrument and began to play a joyful tune full of sunshine and green leaves and summertime. As the music filled the room, Aengus stirred and opened his eyes. Caer smiled, for there was not a white feather to be seen. The hand plucking the strings was that of a young woman.

"Who are you?" Aengus asked, sitting up. But she could not answer him. She played on all through the night while he watched and listened and smiled, as if caught in some deep enchantment.

When the first gray light of dawn crept through the window, Caer's body felt light and her arms began to melt away like a dream. She put the harp down just in time.

"Don't leave!" he cried, but she was already too far away.

She came to Aengus every night after that, and every night she played the harp. Sometimes he would sing. But it grieved Caer that she could not sing with him or answer his questions. She could only smile sadly and play on until dawn.

After many weeks his face grew pale and dark shadows ringed his eyes. One night he could barely raise himself from his bed to watch her.

"Is it love for me that is making him ill?" Caer wondered in alarm.

She put down the harp. He was already asleep when she floated away on the night air.

Although she longed with all her heart to be with Aengus, Caer came to him no more. As winter melted into spring and spring ripened into summer, she remained on the lake with her handmaidens, gliding sadly over the lonely waters.

Aengus's mother, Aífe, noticed the terrible change in her son. He had lost all interest in hunting and feasting. He stayed in his bed all day long.

"Call the best physicians to me," she commanded.

One by one, wise men came to examine Aengus, but none of them could find the cause of his illness. Finally Aífe called Fergne, the most famous physician of all.

Fergne ordered everyone out of the chamber and looked at Aengus's pale face. "I know what this is, Aengus," he said. "You are in love with a woman you have never met."

"You are right," sighed Aengus. "What shall I do? She came to me in my dreams, many times – a girl with eyes like the night and hair like the sun. She made my harp sing like the birds of the Shee. But when dawn came she melted away, and now for months she has not come at all."

"We must find her," said Fergne.

Fergne reported the news to Aífe. She sent messengers from King Leary's court into all parts of Ireland, but in none of them did they find the girl.

They returned to Aífe and reported their failure.

"You have sought the girl only in the dwellings of mortals," said Aífe. "Go, search for her among the immortals, among the kings of the Shee-mounds and the fairy folk, and see if she may be one of them."

The mists of autumn crept over the waters of Loch Bél Dracon and soon it was Samain eve once again. Caer and her companions flew home to Ethal's fortress and descended on the courtyard in a thunder of white wings. As sunset fired the flagstones, their feathers vanished and their human shapes returned.

Caer's mother wrapped her in a warm cloak and hurried her inside. "There are rumors," she whispered, "of a search for a girl with golden hair who plays the harp. Your father is suspicious. Be careful!"

A knot of hope and fear tightened around Caer's heart.

One day, as Caer gazed from her high window, she saw a group of travelers approach the fortress. A servant knocked on her door.

"Messengers have come from King Leary of Ulster," the maid said. "They would speak with you."

Caer's heartbeat quickened as she descended the stairs to the great hall. She bowed to the tall, cloaked men who stood before her mother. Her father was nowhere to be seen.

"Greetings from the court of King Leary," said one of them, looking carefully at her face. "Do you play the harp, my lady?"

"Yes, I do."

"Would you do us the great honor of playing for us?"

Caer glanced at her mother, who nodded quickly and handed her the harp.

Caer's fingers moved across the strings and she played a slow lament, a song so sad it seemed to contain all the heartbreak in the world. The messengers exchanged glances and smiled through the tears that spilled down their cheeks.

"What is this?" Caer's father burst into the room in his hunting attire, eyes blazing. He seized Caer's arm and pushed her away. "Who are you?" he demanded of the visitors.

"We come from the court of King Leary of Ulster, Lord, and we seek a maiden who . . ."

"My daughter is of no interest to you. Now begone, before I work some dark magic upon you all!"

The messengers hurried out of the great hall. Caer fled from her father's rage.

Perhaps, she dared to hope, the travelers had heard enough.

The messengers returned to King Leary's court. "We have found the girl," they told Aífe. "She is the daughter of Ethal of the Shee-mound at Navan."

"Ethal is a powerful sorcerer, and immortal," said Aífe. "He will not easily give up his daughter. He can be killed only by strong magic." She paced the room, brow furrowed. Suddenly, she looked up and smiled. "Go to my old friend the Dagda. He and Ethal are bitter enemies, and he alone possesses magic as strong as Ethal's and has the power to overcome him and save my son's life. Go, quickly!"

Soon a vast army surrounded Ethal's fortress. Spears and flaming brands and rocks hissed through the air, but the fortress was strong and its walls were high.

Then, on Samain eve, a hush fell over the massed warriors. A giant of a man, the Dagda, strode up to the gate. He raised one hand. Lightning crackled overhead. Thunder rumbled. A wintry wind howled across the ramparts.

But it was past sunset, and Caer could remain in human form no longer. She and her handmaidens hurried to the courtyard. They lifted their arms and became swans once again, rising over the ranks of warriors on the plain. Caer saw her father standing outside the gate, facing the Dagda alone. The giant raised his magic club. Ethal held aloft his sorcerer's staff. Lightning flashed between them.

Caer's fate forbade her to linger. With a heavy heart she flew with her companions toward Loch Bél Dracon.

The swans drifted anxiously on the cold waters of the loch, wondering who had won that terrible battle.

On the first day, black clouds brooded on the horizon. Distant thunder growled over Ethal's fortress.

On the second day, the clouds lifted and shafts of sunlight lit the water.

On the third day, Caer saw people approaching the shore.

"Caer!" called a familiar voice.

Her heart leapt. She beat her wings, rose in the air, and landed on the water near the beach.

"Caer!"

It was Aengus!

He was seated on a litter carried by two servants. He was pale and thin, but he looked straight at her and held up a single white feather.

Caer glided nearer.

"She cannot speak in this form," said her mother's voice.

"Her father is dead, yet this curse remains upon her! Who can set her free?" cried Aengus.

"No one can remove this enchantment," said her mother. "But she herself has inherited some of her father's power. She can transfer the curse to others, and grant immortality to whomever she chooses."

"Then let me also be a swan, Caer!" cried Aengus. "Let me share this curse and we will live together always!"

Caer beat her wings in joy and flew to him. Her handmaidens followed and, in a moment, a spiral of white beating wings swirled around Aengus. And then the whirling spiral was gone and twenty maidens danced hand in hand around two white swans. The swans rose in the air and soared over the trees. They circled the lake three times and were gone.

You might still see them even now, on moonlit
nights on Loch Bél Dracon. And if you listen
carefully, every other year, you might hear
the strains of a harp and two voices
singing in the shadowy woods
by the cold, cold shore.